A Beginning-to-Read Book

Happy Birthday, Dear Dragon

by Margaret Hillert
Illustrated by Jack Pullan

NORWOOD HOUSE PRESS

DEAR CAREGIVER,

The books in this Beginning-to-Read collection may look somewhat familiar in that the original versions could have been a part of your own early reading experiences. These carefully written texts feature common sight words to provide your child multiple exposures to the words appearing most frequently in written text. These new versions have been updated and the engaging illustrations are highly appealing to a contemporary audience of young readers.

Begin by reading the story to your child, followed by letting him or her read familiar words and soon your child will be able to read the story independently. At each step of the way, be sure to praise your reader's efforts to build his or her confidence as an independent reader. Discuss the pictures and encourage your child to make connections between the story and his or her own life. At the end of the story, you will find reading activities and a word list that will help your child practice and strengthen beginning reading skills. These activities, along with the comprehension questions are aligned to current standards, so reading efforts at home will directly support the instructional goals in the classroom.

Above all, the most important part of the reading experience is to have fun and enjoy it!

Shannon Cannon

Shannon Cannon,
Literacy Consultant

Norwood House Press • www.norwoodhousepress.com
Beginning-to-Read™ is a registered trademark of Norwood House Press.
Illustration and cover design copyright ©2017 by Norwood House Press. All Rights Reserved.

Authorized adapted reprint from the U.S. English language edition, entitled Happy Birthday, Dear Dragon by Margaret Hillert. Copyright © 2017 Margaret Hillert. Reprinted with permission. All rights reserved. Pearson and Happy Birthday, Dear Dragon are trademarks, in the US and/or other countries, of Pearson Education, Inc. or its affiliates. This publication is protected by copyright, and prior permission to re-use in any way in any format is required by both Norwood House Press and Pearson Education. This book is authorized in the United States for use in schools and public libraries.

LIBRARY OF CONGRESS CATALOGING-IN-PUBLICATION DATA
    Names: Hillert, Margaret, author. | Pullan, Jack, illustrator.
    Title: Happy birthday, Dear Dragon / by Margaret Hillert ; illustrated by Jack Pullan.
    Description: Chicago, IL : Norwood House Press, [2016] | Series: A
        beginning-to-read book | Summary: "A young boy celebrates his birthday and
        receives a pet dragon as a gift. The two play and become the best of
        friends. Completely re-illustrated from original edition. Includes reading
        activities and a word list"-- Provided by publisher.
    Identifiers: LCCN 2015046732 (print) | LCCN 2016014722 (ebook) | ISBN
        9781599537672 (library edition : alk. paper) | ISBN 9781603578936 (eBook)
    Subjects: | CYAC: Birthdays--Fiction. | Dragons--Fiction.
    Classification: LCC PZ7.H558 Hap 2016 (print) | LCC PZ7.H558 (ebook) | DDC
        [E]--dc23
    LC record available at http://lccn.loc.gov/2015046732

288N—072016
Manufactured in the United States of America in North Mankato, Minnesota.

This looks good, Mother.
What a big one.
Oh, this is fun.

Here is something.
What is it?
I can not guess.

Oh, look here.
Look at this
—and this
—and this!

And here is something that can jump up.

Now come with me.
I want to get you something.
Run, run run!

Here we go.
In here. In here.
We will look at dogs.

But we have a dog, Father.
I like the one we have.

Here is something little.
Do you want this?
You can look at it.
It can look at you.

No, I do not want it.
What can it do?
It can not play with me.

Look down here.
You can have this one.
Do you like it?
See it jump.

I like that little one.
But it is not what I want.
Come here.
Come here.

Here is what I want.
Oh, will you get it for me?
I like it.
I like it.
I like it!

Come with me.
Come to my house.
I like you.
We can have fun.

Look, Mother.
See what I have.
It can play with me.

I see.
I see.
It is funny.
We will find something for it.

I want to go for a ride.
I will get in.
Help me.
Help me.

Here we go.
Run, run, run!
What fun!
What fun!

Will you do something for me?
Will you help me with this?

Have one.
Have two.
Have three.
You are a big help.

Oh, my.
Oh, my.
Look what you can do.
I like this!

Here you are with me.
And here I am with you.

Oh, what a happy
birthday, Dear Dragon.

The following activities support the findings of the National Reading Panel that determined the most effective components for reading instruction are: Phonemic Awareness, Phonics, Vocabulary, Fluency, and Text Comprehension.

Phonemic Awareness: The /d/ sound

Sound Substitution: Say the words on the left to your child. Ask your child to repeat the word, changing the first sound to /**d**/:

pot - /d/ = dot	junk - /d/ = dunk	keep - /d/ = deep
bent - /d/ = dent	fish - /d/ = dish	near - /d/ = dear
time - /d/ = dime	kid - /d/ = did	rip - /d/ = dip

Phonics: The letter Dd

1. Demonstrate how to form the letters **D** and **d** for your child.

2. Have your child practice writing **D** and **d** at least three times each.

3. Ask your child to point to the words in the book that start with the letter **d.**

4. Write down the following words and ask your child to circle the letter **d** in each word:

do	dragon	dog	dear	day
food	wood	dad	den	hand
riddle	sad	doll	puddle	dig

Vocabulary: Naming Objects

1. Ask your child to tell you different words he or she thinks of that go with "birthday". Write the words on sticky notes and have the child place them next to any objects he or she has named that are in the story.

2. Ask your child to tell a story using all of the words he or she has come up with that relate to birthday.

Fluency: Echo Reading

1. Reread the story to your child at least two more times while your child tracks the print by running a finger under the words as they are read. Ask your child to read the words he or she knows with you.

2. Reread the story, stopping after each sentence or page to allow your child to read (echo) what you have read. Repeat echo reading and let your child take the lead.

Text Comprehension: Discussion Time

1. Ask your child to retell the sequence of events in the story.

2. To check comprehension, ask your child the following questions:
   - Why didn't the boy want the dog for his birthday?
   - Why didn't the boy want the fish for his birthday?
   - Which parts of this story could really happen?
   - Which parts of this story couldn't really happen?
   - Which pet would you choose? Why?

WORD LIST

Happy Birthday, Dear Dragon uses the 63 words listed below.

This list can be used to practice reading the words that appear in the text. You may wish to write the words on index cards and use them to help your child build automatic word recognition. Regular practice with these words will enhance your child's fluency in reading connected text.

a	Father	I	oh	up
am	find	in	one	
and	for	is		want
are	fun	it	play	we
at	funny			what
		jump	ride	will
big	get		run	with
birthday	go	like		
but	good	little	see	you
	guess	look (s)	something	
can				
come	happy	me	that	
	have	Mother	the	
dear	help	my	this	
do	here		three	
dog (s)	house	no	to	
down		not	two	
dragon		now		

ABOUT THE AUTHOR Margaret Hillert has helped millions of children all over the world learn to read independently. She was a first grade teacher for 34 years and during that time started writing books that her students could both gain confidence in reading and enjoy. She wrote well over 100 books for children just learning to read. As a child, she enjoyed writing poetry and continued her poetic writings as an adult for both children and adults.

Photograph by Glenna Washburn

ABOUT THE ILLUSTRATOR A talented and creative illustrator, Jack Pullan, is a graduate of William Jewell College. He has also studied informally at Oxford University and the Kansas City Art Institute. He was mentored by the renowned watercolor artists, Jim Hamil and Bill Amend. Jack's work has graced the pages of many enjoyable children's books, various educational materials, cartoon strips, as well as many greeting cards. Jack currently resides in Kansas.